Gambler's World

Gambler's World

by Keith Laumer

Wilder Publications, LLC.
PO Box 243
Blacksburg, VA 24060

ISBN 10: 1-60459-653-8
ISBN 13: 978-1-60459-653-3

Table of Contents

Chapter I

Retief paused before a tall mirror to check the overlap of the four sets of lapels that ornamented the vermilion cutaway of a First Secretary and Consul.

"Come along, Retief," Magnan said. "The Ambassador has a word to say to the staff before we go in."

"I hope he isn't going to change the spontaneous speech he plans to make when the Potentate impulsively suggests a trade agreement along the lines they've been discussing for the last two months."

"Your derisive attitude is uncalled for, Retief," Magnan said sharply. "I think you realize it's delayed your promotion in the Corps."

Retief took a last glance in the mirror. "I'm not sure I want a promotion," he said. "It would mean more lapels."

Ambassador Crodfoller pursed his lips, waiting until Retief and Magnan took places in the ring of Terrestrial diplomats around him.

"A word of caution only, gentlemen," he said. "Keep always foremost in your minds the necessity for our identification with the Nenni Caste. Even a hint of familiarity with lower echelons could mean the failure of the mission. Let us remember that the Nenni represent authority here on Petreac. Their traditions must be observed, whatever our personal preferences. Let's go along now. The Potentate will be making his entrance any moment."

Magnan came to Retief's side as they moved toward the salon.

"The Ambassador's remarks were addressed chiefly to you, Retief," he said. "Your laxness in these matters is notorious. Naturally, I believe firmly in democratic principles myself—"

"Have you ever had a feeling, Mr. Magnan, that there's a lot going on here that we don't know about?"

Magnan nodded. "Quite so. Ambassador Crodfoller's point exactly. Matters which are not of concern to the Nenni are of no concern to us."

"Another feeling I get is that the Nenni aren't very bright. Now suppose—"

"I'm not given to suppositions, Retief. We're here to implement the policies of the Chief of Mission. And I should dislike to be in the shoes of a member of the staff whose conduct jeopardized the agreement that will be concluded here tonight."

A bearer with a tray of drinks rounded a fluted column, shied as he confronted the diplomats, fumbled the tray, grabbed and sent a glass crashing to the floor.

Magnan leaped back, slapping at the purple cloth of his pants leg. Retief's hand shot out to steady the tray. The servant rolled terrified eyes.

"I'll take one of these, now that you're here," Retief said. He took a glass from the tray, winking at the servant.

"No harm done," he said. "Mr. Magnan's just warming up for the big dance."

A Nenni major-domo bustled up, rubbing his hands politely.

"Some trouble here?" he said. "What happened, Honorables, what, what...."

"The blundering idiot," Magnan spluttered. "How dare—"

"You're quite an actor, Mr. Magnan," Retief said. "If I didn't know about your democratic principles, I'd think you were really mad."

The servant ducked his head and scuttled away.

"Has this fellow...." The major-domo eyed the retreating bearer.

"I dropped my glass," Retief said. "Mr. Magnan's upset because he hates to see liquor wasted."

Retief turned to find himself face-to-face with Ambassador Crodfoller.

"I witnessed that," The Ambassador hissed. "By the goodness of Providence, the Potentate and his retinue haven't appeared yet. But I can assure you the servants saw it. A more un-Nenni-like display I would find it difficult to imagine!"

Retief arranged his features in an expression of deep interest.

"More un-Nenni-like, sir?" he said. "I'm not sure I—"

"Bah!" The Ambassador glared at Retief, "Your reputation has preceded you, sir. Your name is associated with a number of the most bizarre incidents in Corps history. I'm warning you; I'll tolerate nothing." He turned and stalked away.

"Ambassador-baiting is a dangerous sport, Retief," Magnan said.

Retief took a swallow of his drink. "Still," he said, "it's better than no sport at all."

"Your time would be better spent observing the Nenni mannerisms. Frankly, Retief, you're not fitting into the group at all well."

"I'll be candid with you, Mr. Magnan. The group gives me the willies."

"Oh, the Nenni are a trifle frivolous, I'll concede," Magnan said. "But it's with them that we must deal. And you'd be making a contribution to the overall mission if you merely abandoned that rather arrogant manner of yours." Magnan looked at Retief critically. "You can't help your height, of course. But couldn't you curve your back just a bit—and possibly assume a more placating expression? Just act a little more...."

"Girlish?"

"Exactly." Magnan nodded, then looked sharply at Retief.

Retief drained his glass and put it on a passing tray.

"I'm better at acting girlish when I'm well juiced," he said. "But I can't face another sorghum-and-soda. I suppose it would be un-Nenni-like to slip the bearer a credit and ask for a Scotch and water."

"Decidedly." Magnan glanced toward a sound across the room.

"Ah, here's the Potentate now!" He hurried off.

Retief watched the bearers coming and going, bringing trays laden with drinks, carrying off empties. There was a lull in the drinking now, as the diplomats gathered around the periwigged Chief of State and his courtiers. Bearers loitered near the service door, eyeing the notables. Retief strolled over to the service door, pushed through it into a narrow white-tiled hall filled with the odors of the kitchen. Silent servants gaped as he passed, watching as he moved along to the kitchen door and stepped inside.

Chapter II

A dozen or more low-caste Petreacans, gathered around a long table in the center of the room looked up, startled. A heap of long-bladed bread knives, French knives, carving knives and cleavers lay in the center of the table. Other knives were thrust into belts or held in the hands of the men. A fat man in the yellow sarong of a cook stood frozen in the act of handing a knife to a tall one-eyed sweeper.

Retief took one glance, then let his eyes wander to a far corner of the room. Humming a careless little tune, he sauntered across to the open liquor shelves, selected a garish green bottle and turned unhurriedly back toward the door. The group of servants watched him, transfixed.

As Retief reached the door, it swung inward. Magnan, lips pursed, stood in the doorway.

"I had a premonition," he said.

"I'll bet it was a dandy," Retief said. "You must tell me all about it—in the salon."

"We'll have this out right here," Magnan snapped. "I've warned you!" Magnan's voice trailed off as he took in the scene around the table.

"After you," Retief said, nudging Magnan toward the door.

"What's going on here?" Magnan barked. He stared at the men, started around Retief. A hand stopped him.

"Let's be going," Retief said, propelling Magnan toward the hall.

"Those knives!" Magnan yelped. "Take your hands off me, Retief! What are you men—?"

Retief glanced back. The fat cook gestured suddenly, and the men faded back. The cook stood, arm cocked, a knife across his palm.

"Close the door and make no sound," he said softly.

Magnan pressed back against Retief. "Let's ... r-run...." he faltered.

Retief turned slowly, put his hands up.

"I don't run very well with a knife in my back," he said. "Stand very still, Magnan, and do just what he tells you."

"Take them out through the back," the cook said.

"What does he mean?" Magnan spluttered. "Here, you—"

"Silence," the cook said, almost casually. Magnan gaped at him, closed his mouth.

Two of the men with knives came to Retief's side and gestured, grinning broadly.

"Let's go, peacocks," one said.

Retief and Magnan silently crossed the kitchen, went out the back door, stopped on command and stood waiting. The sky was brilliant with stars. A gentle breeze stirred the tree-tops beyond the garden. Behind them the servants talked in low voices.

"You go too, Illy," the cook was saying.

"Do it here," another said.

"And carry their damn dead bodies down?"

"Pitch 'em behind the hedge."

"I said the river. Three of you is plenty for a couple of Nenni. We don't know if we want to—"

"They're foreigners, not Nenni. We don't know—"

"So they're foreign Nenni. Makes no difference. I've seen them. I need every man here; now get going."

"What about the big guy? He looks tough."

"Him? He waltzed into the room and didn't notice a thing. But watch the other one."

At a prod from a knife point, Retief moved off down the walk, two of the escort behind him and Magnan, another going ahead to scout the way.

Magnan moved closer to Retief.

"Say," he said in a whisper. "That fellow in the lead; isn't he the one who spilled the drink? The one you took the blame for?"

"That's him, all right. He doesn't seem nervous any more, I notice."

"You saved him from serious punishment," Magnan said. "He'll be grateful; he'll let us go."

"Better check with the fellows with the knives before you act on that."

"Say something to him," Magnan hissed, "Remind him."

The lead man fell back in line with Retief and Magnan.

"These two are scared of you," he said, grinning and jerking a thumb toward the knife-handlers. "They haven't worked around the Nenni like me; they don't know you."

"Don't you recognize this gentleman?" Magnan said.

"He did me a favor," the man said. "I remember."

"What's it all about?" Retief asked.

"The revolution. We're taking over now."

"Who's 'we'?"

"The People's Anti-Fascist Freedom League."

"What are all the knives for?"

"For the Nenni; and for all you foreigners."

"What do you mean?" Magnan gasped.

"We'll slit all the throats at one time. Saves a lot of running around."

"What time will that be?"

"Just at dawn; and dawn comes early, this time of year. By full daylight the PAFFL will be in charge."

"You'll never succeed," Magnan said. "A few servants with knives! You'll all be caught and killed."

"By who, the Nenni?" the man laughed. "You Nenni are a caution."

"But we're not Nenni—"

"We've watched you; you're the same. You're part of the same blood-sucking class."

"There are better ways to, uh, adjust differences," Magnan said. "This killing won't help you, I'll personally see to it that your grievances are heard in the Corps Courts. I can assure you that the plight of the downtrodden workers will be alleviated. Equal rights for all—"

"These threats won't work," the man said. "You don't scare me."

"Threats? I'm promising relief to the exploited classes of Petreac!"

"You must be nuts," the man said. "You trying to upset the system or something?"

"Isn't that the purpose of your revolution?"

"Look, Nenni, we're tired of you Nenni getting all the graft. We want our turn. What good would it do us to run Petreac if there's no loot?"

"You mean you intend to oppress the people? But they're your own group."

"Group, schmoop. We're taking all the chances; we're doing the work. We deserve the payoff. You think we're throwing up good jobs for the fun of it?"

"You're basing a revolt on these cynical premises?"

"Wise up, Nenni. There's never been a revolution for any other reason."

"Who's in charge of this?" Retief said.

"Shoke, the head chef."

"I mean the big boss. Who tells Shoke what all to do?"

"Oh, that's Zorn. Look out, here's where we start down the slope. It's slippery."

"Look," Magnan said. "You."

"My name's Illy."

"Mr. Illy, this man showed you mercy when he could have had you beaten."

"Keep moving. Yeah, I said I was grateful."

"Yes," Magnan said, swallowing hard. "A noble emotion, gratitude. You won't regret it."

"I always try to pay back a good turn," Illy said. "Watch your step now on this sea-wall."

"You'll never regret it," Magnan said.

"This is far enough," Illy motioned to one of the knife men. "Give me your knife, Vug."

The man passed his knife to Illy. There was an odor of sea-mud and kelp. Small waves slapped against the stones of the sea-wall. The wind was stronger here.

"I know a neat stroke," Illy said. "Practically painless. Who's first?"

"What do you mean?" Magnan quavered.

"I said I was grateful. I'll do it myself, give you a nice clean job. You know these amateurs; botch it up and have a guy floppin' around, yellin' and spatterin' everybody up."

"I'm first," Retief said. He pushed past Magnan, stopped suddenly, drove a straight punch at Illy's mouth.

The long blade flicked harmlessly over Retief's shoulder as Illy fell. Retief whirled, leaped past Magnan, took the unarmed servant by the throat and belt, lifted him and slammed him against the third man. Both scrambled, yelped and fell from the sea-wall into the water.

Retief turned back to Illy. He pulled off the man's belt and strapped his hands together.

Magnan found his voice.

"You.... we.... they...."

"I know," Retief said.

"We've got to get back," Magnan said, "Warn them!"

"We'd never get through the rebel cordon around the palace. And if we did, trying to give an alarm would only set the assassinations off early."

"We can't just...."

"We've got to go to the source; this fellow Zorn. Get him to call it off."

"We'd be killed! At least we're safe here."

Illy groaned and opened his eyes. He sat up.

"On your feet, Illy," Retief said.

Illy looked around. "I'm sick," he said.

"The damp air is bad for you. Let's be going." Retief pulled the man to his feet. "Where does Zorn stay when he's in town?" he demanded.

"What happened? Where's Vug and...."

"They had an accident. Fell in the pond."

Illy gazed down at the restless black water.

"I guess I had you Nenni figured wrong."

"Us Nenni have hidden qualities. Let's get moving before Vug and Slug make it to shore and start it all over again."

"No hurry," Illy said. "They can't swim." He spat into the water. "So long, Vug. So long, Toscin. Take a pull, at the Hell Horn for me." He started off along the sea wall toward the sound of the surf.

"You want to see Zorn, I'll take you to see Zorn," he said. "I can't swim either."

Chapter III

"I take it," Retief said, "that the casino is a front for his political activities."

"He makes plenty off it. This PAFFL is a new kick. I never heard about it until maybe a couple months ago."

Retief motioned toward a dark shed with an open door.

"We'll stop here," he said, "long enough to strip the gadgets off these uniforms."

Illy, hands strapped behind his back, stood by and watched as Retief and Magnan removed medals, ribbons, orders and insignia from the formal diplomatic garments.

"This may help some," Retief said, "if the word is out that two diplomats are loose."

"It's a breeze," Illy said. "We see cats in purple and orange tailcoats all the time."

"I hope you're right," Retief said. "But if we're called, you'll be the first to go, Illy."

"You're a funny kind of Nenni," Illy said, eyeing Retief, "Toscin and Vug must be wonderin' what happened to 'em."

"If you think I'm good at drowning people, you ought to see me with a knife. Let's get going."

"It's only a little way now," Illy said. "But you better untie me. Somebody's liable to stick their nose in and get me killed."

"I'll take the chance. How do we get to the casino?"

"We follow this street. It twists around and goes under a couple tunnels. When we get to the Drunkard's Stairs we go up and it's right in front of us. A pink front with a sign like a big Luck Wheel."

"Give me your belt, Magnan," Retief said.

Magnan handed it over.

"Lie down, Illy," Retief said.

The servant looked at Retief.

"Vug and Toscin will be glad to see me," he said. "But they'll never believe me." He lay down. Retief strapped his feet together and stuffed a handkerchief in his mouth.

"Why are you doing that?" Magnan asked. "We need him."

"We know the way. And we don't need anyone to announce our arrival. It's only on three-dee that you can march a man through a gang of his pals with a finger in his back."

Magnan looked at the man. "Maybe you'd better, uh, cut his throat," he said.

Illy rolled his eyes.

"That's a very un-Nenni-like suggestion, Mr. Magnan," Retief said. "If we have any trouble finding the casino, I'll give it serious thought."

There were few people in the narrow street. Shops were shuttered, windows dark.

"Maybe they heard about the coup," Magnan said. "They're lying low."

"More likely, they're at the palace picking up their knives."

They rounded a corner, stepped over a man curled in the gutter snoring heavily and found themselves at the foot of a long flight of littered stone steps.

"The Drunkard's Stairs are plainly marked," Magnan sniffed.

"I hear sounds up there," Retief said. "Sounds of merrymaking."

"Maybe we'd better go back."

"Merrymaking doesn't scare me," Retief said. "Come to think of it, I don't know what the word means." He started up, Magnan behind him.

At the top of the long stair a dense throng milled in the alley-like street.

A giant illuminated roulette wheel revolved slowly above them. A loudspeaker blared the chant of the croupiers from the tables inside. Magnan and Retief moved through the crowd toward the wide-open doors.

Magnan plucked at Retief's sleeve. "Are you sure we ought to push right in like this? Maybe we ought to wait a bit, look around...."

"When you're where you have no business being," Retief said, "always stride along purposefully. If you loiter, people begin to get curious."

Inside, a mob packed the wide, low-ceilinged room, clustered around gambling devices in the form of towers, tables and basins.

"What do we do now?" Magnan asked.

"We gamble. How much money do you have in your pockets?"

"Why ... a few credits." Magnan handed the money to Retief. "But what about the man Zorn?"

"A purple cutaway is conspicuous enough, without ignoring the tables," Retief said. "We've got a hundred credits between us. We'll get to Zorn in due course, I hope."

"Your pleasure, gents," a bullet-headed man said, eyeing the colorful evening clothes of the diplomats. "You'll be wantin' to try your luck at the Zoop tower, I'd guess. A game for real sporting gents."

"Why ... ah ..." Magnan said.

"What's a zoop tower?" Retief asked.

"Out-of-towners, hey?" The bullet-headed man shifted his dope-stick to the other corner of his mouth. "Zoop is a great little game. Two teams of players buy into the pot. Each player takes a lever;

the object is to make the ball drop from the top of the tower into your net. Okay?"

"What's the ante?"

"I got a hundred-credit pot workin' now, gents."

Retief nodded. "We'll try it."

The shill led the way to an eight-foot tower mounted on gimbals. Two perspiring men in trade-class pullovers gripped two of the levers that controlled the tilt of the tower. A white ball lay in a hollow in the thick glass platform at the top. From the center, an intricate pattern of grooves led out to the edge of the glass. Retief and Magnan took chairs before the two free levers.

"When the light goes on, gents, work the lever to jack the tower. You got three gears. Takes a good arm to work top gear. That's this button here. The little knob controls what way you're goin'. May the best team win. I'll take the hundred credits now."

Retief handed over the money. A red light flashed on, and Retief tried the lever.

It moved easily, with a ratcheting sound. The tower trembled, slowly tilted toward the two perspiring workmen pumping frantically at their levers. Magnan started slowly, accelerated as he saw the direction the tower was taking.

"Faster, Retief," he said. "They're winning."

"This is against the clock, gents," the bullet-headed man said. "If nobody wins when the light goes off, the house takes all."

"Crank it over to the left," Retief said.

"I'm getting tired."

"Shift to a lower gear."

The tower leaned. The ball stirred, rolled into a concentric channel. Retief shifted to middle gear, worked the lever. The tower creaked to a stop, started back upright.

"There isn't any lower gear," Magnan gasped. One of the two on the other side of the tower shifted to middle gear; the other followed suit. They worked harder now, heaving against the stiff levers. The tower quivered, moved slowly toward their side.

"I'm exhausted," Magnan gasped. He dropped the lever, lolled back in the chair, gulping air. Retief shifted position, took Magnan's lever with his left hand.

"Shift it to middle gear," Retief said. Magnan gulped, punched the button and slumped back, panting.

"My arm," he said. "I've injured myself."

The two men in pullovers conferred hurriedly as they cranked their levers; then one punched a button and the other reached across, using his left arm to help.

"They've shifted to high," Magnan said. "Give up, it's hopeless."

"Shift me to high," Retief said. "Both buttons!"

Magnan complied. Retief's shoulders bulged. He brought one lever down, then the other, alternately, slowly at first, then faster. The tower jerked, tilted toward him, farther.... The ball rolled in the channel, found an outlet—

Abruptly, both Retief's levers froze.

The tower trembled, wavered and moved back. Retief heaved. One lever folded at the base, bent down and snapped off short. Retief braced his feet, took the other lever with both hands and pulled.

There was a rasp of metal friction, and a loud twang. The lever came free, a length of broken cable flopping into view. The tower fell over as the two on the other side scrambled aside.

"Hey!" Bullet-head yelled. "You wrecked my equipment!"

Retief got up and faced him.

"Does Zorn know you've got your tower rigged for suckers?"

"You tryin' to call me a cheat or something?"

The crowd had fallen back, ringing the two men. Bullet-head glanced around. With a lightning motion, he plucked a knife from somewhere.

"That'll be five hundred credits for the equipment," he said. "Nobody calls Kippy a cheat."

Retief picked up the broken lever.

"Don't make me hit you with this, you cheap chiseler."

Kippy looked at the bar.

"Comin' in here," he said indignantly, looking to the crowd for support. "Bustin' up my rig, callin' names...."

"I want a hundred credits," Retief said. "Now."

"Highway robbery!" Kippy yelled.

"Better pay up," somebody called.

"Hit him, mister," someone else said.

A broad-shouldered man with graying hair pushed through the crowd and looked around. "You heard 'em, Kippy. Give," he said.

The shill growled but tucked his knife away. Reluctantly he peeled a bill from a fat roll and handed it over.

The newcomer looked from Retief to Magnan.

"Pick another game, strangers," he said. "Kippy made a little mistake."

"This is small-time stuff," Retief said. "I'm interested in something big."

The broad-shouldered man lit a perfumed dope stick. "What would you call big?" he said softly.

"What's the biggest you've got?"

The man narrowed his eyes, smiling. "Maybe you'd like to try Slam."

"Tell me about it."

"Over here." The crowd opened up, made a path. Retief and Magnan followed across the room to a brightly-lit glass-walled box.

There was an arm-sized opening at waist height. Inside was a hand grip. A two-foot plastic globe a quarter full of chips hung in the center. Apparatus was mounted at the top of the box.

"Slam pays good odds," the man said. "You can go as high as you like. Chips cost you a hundred

credits. You start it up by dropping a chip in here."
He indicated a slot.

"You take the hand grip. When you squeeze, it unlocks. The globe starts to turn. You can see, it's full of chips. There's a hole at the top. As long as you hold the grip, the bowl turns. The harder you squeeze, the faster it turns. Eventually it'll turn over to where the hole is down, and chips fall out.

"On the other hand, there's contact plates spotted around the bowl. When one of 'em lines up with a live contact, you get quite a little jolt—guaranteed nonlethal. All you've got to do is hold on long enough, and you'll get the payoff."

"How often does this random pattern put the hole down?"

"Anywhere from three minutes to fifteen, with the average run of players. Oh, by the way, one more thing. That lead block up there—" The man motioned with his head toward a one-foot cube suspended by a thick cable. "It's rigged to drop every now and again. Averages five minutes. A warning light flashes first. You can take a chance; sometimes the light's a bluff. You can set the clock back on it by dropping another chip—or you can let go the grip."

Retief looked at the massive block of metal.

"That would mess up a man's dealing hand, wouldn't it?"

"The last two jokers who were too cheap to feed the machine had to have 'em off. Their arms, I mean. That lead's heavy stuff."

"I don't suppose your machine has a habit of getting stuck, like Kippy's?"

The broad-shouldered man frowned.

"You're a stranger," he said, "You don't know any better."

"It's a fair game, Mister," someone called.

"Where do I buy the chips?"

The man smiled. "I'll fix you up. How many?"

"One."

"A big spender, eh?" The man snickered, but handed over a large plastic chip.

Chapter IV

Retief stepped to the machine, dropped the coin.

"If you want to change your mind," the man said, "you can back out now. All it'll cost you is the chip you dropped."

Retief reached through the hole, took the grip. It was leather padded hand-filling. He squeezed it. There was a click and bright lights sprang up. The crowd ah!-ed. The globe began to twirl lazily. The four-inch hole at its top was plainly visible.

"If ever the hole gets in position it will empty very quickly," Magnan said, hopefully.

Suddenly, a brilliant white light flooded the glass cage. A sound went up from the spectators.

"Quick, drop a chip," someone called.

"You've only got ten seconds...."

"Let go!" Magnan yelped.

Retief sat silent, holding the grip, frowning up at the weight. The globe twirled faster now. Then the bright white light winked off.

"A bluff!" Magnan gasped.

"That's risky, stranger," the gray-templed man said.

The globe was turning rapidly now, oscillating from side to side. The hole seemed to travel in a wavering loop, dipping lower, swinging up high, then down again.

"It has to move to the bottom soon," Magnan said. "Slow it down."

"The slower it goes, the longer it takes to get to the bottom," someone said.

There was a crackle and Retief stiffened. Magnan heard a sharp intake of breath. The globe slowed, and Retief shook his head, blinking.

The broad-shouldered man glanced at a meter.

"You took pretty near a full jolt, that time," he said.

The hole in the globe was tracing an oblique course now, swinging to the center, then below.

"A little longer," Magnan said.

"That's the best speed I ever seen on the Slam ball," someone said. "How much longer can he hold it?"

Magnan looked at Retief's knuckles. They showed white against the grip. The globe tilted farther, swung around, then down; two chips fell out, clattered down a chute and into a box.

"We're ahead," Magnan said. "Let's quit."

Retief shook his head. The globe rotated, dipped again; three chips fell.

"She's ready," someone called.

"It's bound to hit soon," another voice added excitedly. "Come on, Mister!"

"Slow down," Magnan said. "So it won't move past too quickly."

"Speed it up, before that lead block gets you," someone called.

The hole swung high, over the top, then down the side. Chips rained out of the hole, six, eight....

"Next pass," a voice called.

The white light flooded the cage. The globe whirled; the hole slid over the top, down, down.... A chip fell, two more....

Retief half rose, clamped his jaw and crushed the grip. Sparks flew. The globe slowed, chips spewing. It stopped, swung back, weighted by the mass of chips at the bottom, and stopped again with the hole centered.

illustration

Chips cascaded down the chute, filled the box before Retief, spilled on the floor. The crowd yelled.

Retief released the grip and withdrew his arm at the same instant that the lead block slammed down.

"Good lord," Magnan said. "I felt that through the floor."

Retief turned to the broad-shouldered man.

"This game's all right for beginners," he said. "But I'd like to talk a really big gamble. Why don't we go to your office, Mr. Zorn?"

"Your proposition interests me," Zorn said, grinding out the stump of his dope stick in a brass ashtray. "But there's some angles to this I haven't mentioned yet."

"You're a gambler, Zorn, not a suicide," Retief said. "Take what I've offered. The other idea was fancier, I agree, but it won't work."

"How do I know you birds aren't lying?" Zorn snarled. He stood up, strode up and down the room. "You walk in here and tell me I'll have a task force on my neck, that the Corps won't recognize my regime. Maybe you're right. But I've got other contacts. They say different." He whirled, stared at Retief.

"I have pretty good assurance that once I put it over, the Corps will have to recognize me as the legal government of Petreac. They won't meddle in internal affairs."

"Nonsense," Magnan spoke up. "The Corps will never deal with a pack of criminals calling themselves—"

"Watch your language, you!" Zorn rasped.

"I'll admit Mr. Magnan's point is a little weak," Retief said. "But you're overlooking something. You plan to murder a dozen or so officers of the Corps Diplomatique Terrestrienne along with the local wheels. The corps won't overlook that. It can't."

"Their tough luck they're in the middle," Zorn muttered.

"Our offer is extremely generous, Mr. Zorn," Magnan said. "The post you'll get will pay you very well indeed. As against the certain failure of your planned coup, the choice should be simple."

Zorn eyed Magnan. "Offering me a job—it sounds phony as hell. I thought you birds were goody-goody diplomats."

"It's time you knew," Retief said. "There's no phonier business in the Galaxy than diplomacy."

"You'd better take it, Mr. Zorn," Magnan said.

"Don't push me, Junior!" Zorn said. "You two walk into my headquarters empty-handed and big-mouthed. I don't know what I'm talking to you for. The answer is no. N-I-X, no!"

"Who are you afraid of?" Retief said softly.

Zorn glared at him.

"Where do you get that 'afraid' routine? I'm top man here!"

"Don't kid around, Zorn. Somebody's got you under their thumb. I can see you squirming from here."

"What if I let your boys alone?" Zorn said suddenly. "The Corps won't have anything to say then, huh?"

"The Corps has plans for Petreac, Zorn. You aren't part of them. A revolution right now isn't part of them. Having the Potentate and the whole Nenni caste slaughtered isn't part of them. Do I make myself clear?"

"Listen," Zorn said urgently, pulling a chair around. "I'll tell you guys a few things. You ever heard of a world they call Rotune?"

"Certainly," Magnan said. "It's a near neighbor of yours. Another backward—that is, emergent—"

"Okay," Zorn said. "You guys think I'm a piker, do you? Well, let me wise you up. The Federal Junta on Rotune is backing my play. I'll be recognized by Rotune, and the Rotune fleet will stand by in case I need any help. I'll present the CDT with what you call a fait accompli."

"What does Rotune get out of this? I thought they were your traditional enemies."

"Don't get me wrong. I've got no use for Rotune; but our interests happen to coincide right now."

"Do they?" Retief smiled grimly. "You can spot a sucker as soon as he comes through that door out there—but you go for a deal like this!"

"What do you mean?" Zorn looked angrily at Retief. "It's fool-proof."

"After you get in power, you'll be fast friends with Rotune, is that it?"

"Friends, hell! Just give me time to get set, and I'll square a few things with that—"

"Exactly. And what do you suppose they have in mind for you?"

"What are you getting at?"

"Why is Rotune interested in your take-over?"

Zorn studied Retief's face. "I'll tell you why," he said. "It's you birds. You and your trade agreement. You're here to tie Petreac into some kind of trade combine. That cuts Rotune out. Well, we're doing all right out here. We don't need any commitments to a lot of fancy-pants on the other side of the Galaxy."

"That's what Rotune has sold you, eh?" Retief said, smiling.

"Sold, nothing!"

Zorn ground out his dope-stick, lit another. He snorted angrily.

"Okay; what's your idea?" he asked after a moment.

"You know what Petreac is getting in the way of imports as a result of the agreement?"

"Sure. A lot of junk."

"To be specific," Retief said, "there'll be 50,000 Tatone B-3 dry washers; 100,000 Glo-float motile lamps; 100,000 Earthworm Minor garden cultivators; 25,000 Veco space heaters; and 75,000 replacement elements for Ford Monomeg drives."

"Like I said. A lot of junk."

Retief leaned back, looking sardonically at Zorn, "Here's the gimmick, Zorn," he said. "The Corps is getting a little tired of Petreac and Rotune carrying on their two-penny war out here. Your privateers have a nasty habit of picking on innocent bystanders. After studying both sides, the Corps has decided Petreac would be a little easier to do business with. So this trade agreement was worked out. The Corps can't openly sponsor an arms shipment to a belligerent. But personal appliances are another story."

"So what do we do—plow 'em under with back-yard cultivators?" Zorn looked at Retief, puzzled. "What's the point?"

"You take the sealed monitor unit from the washer, the repeller field generator from the lamp, the converter control from the cultivator, et cetera, et cetera. You fit these together according to some very simple instructions. Presto! You have one hundred thousand Standard-class Y hand blasters. Just the thing to turn the tide in a stalemated war fought with obsolete arms."

"Good lord!" Magnan said. "Retief, are you—"

"I have to tell him," Retief said. "He has to know what he's putting his neck into."

"Weapons, hey?" Zorn said. "And Rotune knows about it?"

"Sure they know about it. It's not too hard to figure out. And there's more. They want the CDT delegation included in the massacre for a reason. It will put Petreac out of the picture; the trade agreement will go to Rotune; and you and your new regime will find yourselves looking down the muzzles of your own blasters."

Zorn threw his dope-stick to the floor with a snarl.

"I should have smelled something when that Rotune smoothie made his pitch." Zorn looked at his watch.

"I've got two hundred armed men in the palace. We've got about forty minutes to get over there before the rocket goes up."

Chapter V

"You'd better stay here on this terrace out of the way until I've spread the word," Zorn said. "Just in case."

"Let me caution you against any ... ah ... slip-ups, Mr. Zorn," Magnan said. "The Nenni are not to be molested—"

Zorn looked at Retief.

"Your friend talks too much," he said. "I'll keep my end of it. He'd better keep his."

"Nothing's happened yet, you're sure?" Magnan said.

"I'm sure," Zorn said. "Ten minutes to go. Plenty of time."

"I'll just step into the salon to assure myself that all is well," Magnan said.

"Suit yourself," Zorn said. "Just stay clear of the kitchen, or you'll get your throat cut." He sniffed at his dope-stick. "What's keeping Shoke?" he muttered.

Magnan stepped to a tall glass door, eased it open and poked his head through the heavy draperies. As he moved to draw back, a voice was faintly audible. Magnan paused, head still through the drapes.

"What's going on there?" Zorn rasped. He and Retief stepped up behind Magnan.

"—breath of air, ha-ha," Magnan was saying.

"Well, come along, Magnan!" Ambassador Crodfoller's voice snapped.

Magnan shifted from one foot to the other then pushed through the drapes.

"Where've you been, Mr. Magnan?" The Ambassador's voice was sharp.

"Oh ... ah ... a slight accident, Mr. Ambassador."

"What's happened to your shoes? Where are your insignia and decorations?"

"I—ah—spilled a drink on them. Sir. Ah—listen...."

The sound of an orchestra came up suddenly, blaring a fanfare.

Zorn shifted restlessly, ear against the glass.

"What's your friend pulling?" he rasped. "I don't like this."

"Keep cool, Zorn," Retief said. "Mr. Magnan is doing a little emergency salvage on his career."

The music died away with a clatter.

"—My God," Ambassador Crodfoller's voice was faint. "Magnan, you'll be knighted for this. Thank God you reached me. Thank God it's not too late. I'll find some excuse. I'll get a gram off at once."

"But you—"

"It's all right, Magnan. You were in time. Another ten minutes and the agreement would have been signed and transmitted. The wheels would have been put in motion. My career ruined...."

Retief felt a prod at his back. He turned.

"Doublecrossed," Zorn said softly. "So much for the word of a diplomat."

Retief looked at the short-barreled needler in Zorn's hand.

"I see you hedge your bets, Zorn," he said.

"We'll wait here," Zorn said, "until the excitement's over inside. I wouldn't want to attract any attention right now."

"Your politics are still lousy, Zorn. The picture hasn't changed. Your coup hasn't got a chance."

"Skip it. I'll take up one problem at a time."

"Magnan's mouth has a habit of falling open at the wrong time—"

"That's my good luck that I heard it. So there'll be no agreement, no guns, no fat job for Tammany Zorn, hey? Well, I can still play it the other way, What have I got to lose?"

With a movement too quick to follow, Retief's hand chopped down across Zorn's wrist. The needler clattered as Zorn reeled, and then Retief's hand clamped Zorn's arm and whirled him around.

"In answer to your last question," Retief said, "your neck."

"You haven't got a chance, doublecrosser," Zorn gasped.

"Shoke will be here in a minute," Retief said. "Tell him it's all off."

"Twist harder, Mister," Zorn said. "Break it off at the shoulder. I'm telling him nothing!"

"The kidding's over, Zorn," Retief said. "Call it off or I'll kill you."

"I believe you," Zorn said. "But you won't have long to remember it."

"All the killing will be for nothing," Retief said. "You'll be dead and the Rotunes will step into the power vacuum."

"So what? When I die, the world ends."

"Suppose I make you another offer, Zorn?"

"Why would it be any better than the last one, chiseler?"

Retief released Zorn's arm, pushed him away, stooped and picked up the needler.

"I could kill you, Zorn. You know that."

"Go ahead!"

Retief reversed the needler, held it out.

"I'm a gambler too, Zorn. I'm gambling you'll listen to what I have to say."

Zorn snatched the gun, stepped back. He looked at Retief.

"That wasn't the smartest bet you ever made, Mister; but go ahead. You've got maybe ten seconds."

"Nobody doublecrossed you, Zorn. Magnan put his foot in it. Too bad. Is that a reason to kill yourself and a lot of other people who've bet their lives on you?"

"They gambled and lost. Tough."

"Maybe you haven't lost yet—if you don't quit."

"Get to the point!"

Retief spoke earnestly for a minute and a half. Zorn stood, gun aimed, listening. Then both men turned as footsteps approached along the terrace. A fat man in a yellow sarong padded up to Zorn.

Zorn tucked the needler in his waistband.

"Hold everything, Shoke," he said. "Tell the boys to put the knives away. Spread the word fast. It's all off."

"I want to commend you, Retief," Ambassador Crodfoller said expansively. "You mixed very well at last night's affair. Actually, I was hardly aware of your presence."

"I've been studying Mr. Magnan's work," Retief said.

"A good man, Magnan. In a crowd, he's virtually invisible."

"He knows when to disappear all right."

"This has been in many ways a model operation, Retief." The Ambassador patted his paunch contentedly. "By observing local social customs and blending harmoniously with the court, I've succeeded in establishing a fine, friendly, working relationship with the Potentate."

"I understand the agreement has been postponed."

The Ambassador chuckled. "The Potentate's a crafty one. Through ... ah ... a special study I have been conducting, I learned last night that he had hoped to, shall I say, 'put one over' on the Corps."

"Great heavens," Retief said.

"Naturally, this placed me in a difficult position. It was my task to quash this gambit, without giving any indication that I was aware of its existence."

"A hairy position indeed," Retief said.

"Quite casually, I informed the Potentate that certain items which had been included in the terms of the agreement had been deleted and others substituted. I admired him at that moment, Retief. He took it coolly—appearing completely indifferent—perfectly dissembling his very serious disappointment."

"I noticed him dancing with three girls wearing a bunch of grapes apiece. He's very agile for a man of his bulk."

"You mustn't discount the Potentate! Remember, beneath that mask of frivolity, he had absorbed a bitter blow."

"He had me fooled," Retief said.

"Don't feel badly; I confess at first I failed to sense his shrewdness." The Ambassador nodded and moved off along the corridor.

Retief turned and went into an office. Magnan looked up from his desk.

"Ah," he said. "Retief. I've been meaning to ask you. About the ... ah ... blasters. Are you—?"

Retief leaned on Magnan's desk, looked at him.

"I thought that was to be our little secret."

"Well, naturally I—" Magnan closed his mouth, swallowed. "How is it, Retief," he said sharply, "that you were aware of this blaster business, when the Ambassador himself wasn't?"

"Easy," Retief said. "I made it up."

"You what!" Magnan looked wild. "But the agreement—it's been revised! Ambassador Crodfoller has gone on record...."

"Too bad. Glad I didn't tell him about it."

Magnan leaned back and closed his eyes.

"It was big of you to take all the ... blame," Retief said, "when the Ambassador was talking about knighting people."

Magnan opened his eyes.

"What about that gambler, Zorn? Won't he be upset?"

"It's all right," Retief said, "I made another arrangement. The business about making blasters out of common components wasn't completely imaginary. You can actually do it, using parts from an old-fashioned disposal unit."

"What good will that do him?" Magnan whispered, looking nervous. "We're not shipping in any old-fashioned disposal units."

"We don't need to," Retief said. "They're already installed in the palace kitchen—and in a few thousand other places, Zorn tells me."

"If this ever leaks...." Magnan put a hand to his forehead.

"I have his word on it that the Nenni slaughter is out. This place is ripe for a change. Maybe Zorn is what it needs."

"But how can we know?" Magnan yelped. "How can we be sure?"

"We can't," Retief said. "But it's not up to the Corps to meddle in Petreacs' internal affairs." He leaned over, picked up Magnan's desk lighter and lit a cigar. He blew a cloud of smoke toward the ceiling. "Right?"

Magnan looked at him, nodded weakly. "Right."

"I'd better be getting along to my desk," Retief said. "Now that the Ambassador feels that I'm settling down at last—"

"Retief," Magnan said, "tonight, I implore you. Stay out of the kitchen—no matter what."

Retief raised his eyebrows.

"I know," Magnan said. "If you hadn't interfered, we'd all have had our throats cut. But at least," he added, "we'd have died in accordance with regulations!"

Printed in Great Britain
by Amazon

80091080R00031